# Dogs

## The Sound of D

By Alice K. Flanagan

The Child's World®, Inc.

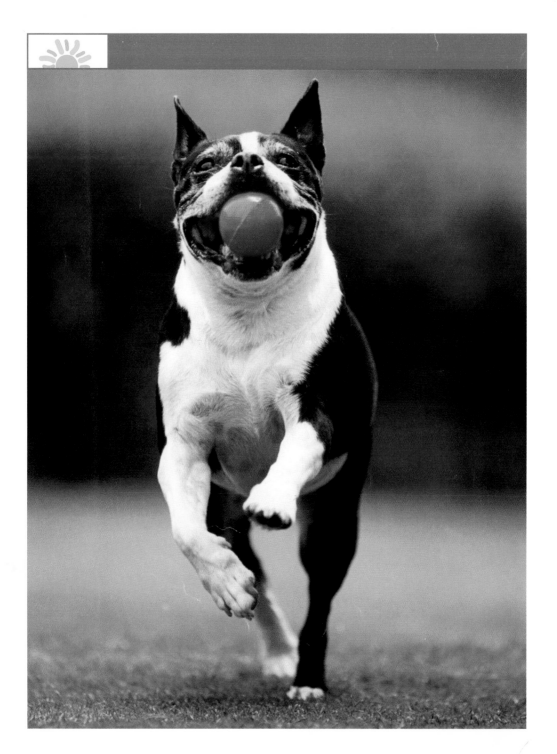

2

Some dogs run after balls.

Some dogs come when they are called.

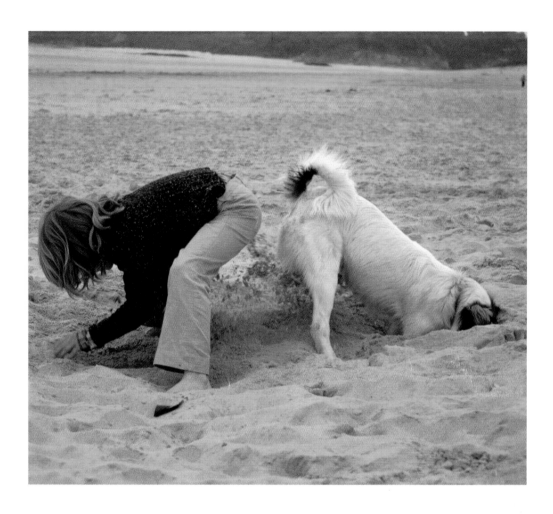

Some dogs dig in
the sand.

Some dogs take baths in a tub.

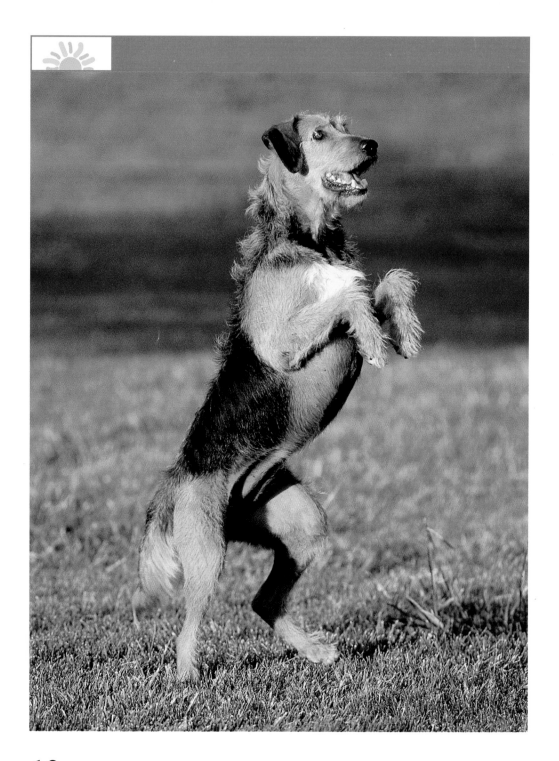

Some dogs walk on two legs.

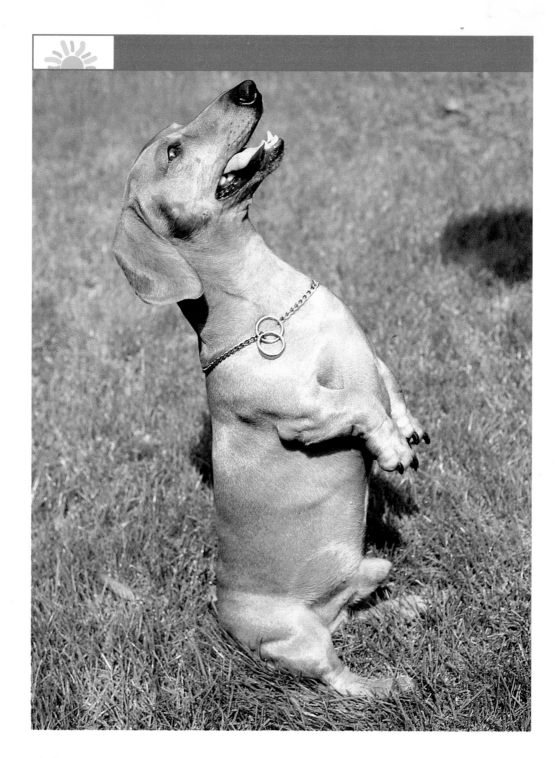

Some dogs jump and some can beg.

Some dogs nap on
a rug.

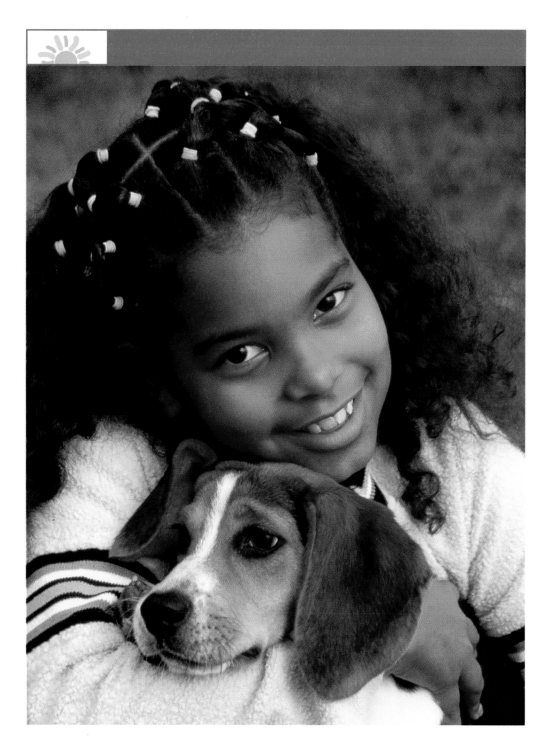

16

Some dogs get lots
of hugs.

Some dogs help us if they can.

Dogs can be our best friends.

# Word List

dig

dogs

# Note to Parents and Educators

The books in the Phonics series of the Wonder Books are based on current research which supports the idea that our brains are pattern detectors rather than rules appliers. This means children learn to read easier when they are taught the familiar spelling patterns found in English. As children encounter more complex words, they have greater success in figuring out these words by using the spelling patterns.

Throughout the 35 books, the texts provide the reader with the opportunity to practice and apply knowledge of the sounds in natural language. The 10 books on the long and short vowels introduce the sounds using familiar onsets and rimes, or spelling patterns, for reinforcement. For example, the word "cat" might be used to present the short "a" sound, with the letter "c" being the onset and "-at" being the rime. This approach provides practice and reinforcement of the short "a" sound, as there are many familiar words made with the "-at" rime.

The 21 consonants and the 4 blends ("ch," "sh," "th," and "wh") use many of these same rimes. The letter(s) before the vowel in a word are considered the onset. Changing the onset allows the consonant books in the series to maintain the practice and reinforcement of the rimes. The repeated use of a word or phrase reinforces the target sound.

The numbers on the spine of each the book facilitate arranging the books in the order that children acquire each sound. The books can also be arranged into groups of long vowels, short vowels, consonants, and blends. All the books in each grouping have their numbers printed in the same color on the spine. The books can be grouped and regrouped easily and quickly, depending on the teacher's needs.

The stories and accompanying photographs in this series are based on time-honored concepts in children's literature: Well-written, engaging texts and colorful, high-quality photographs combine to produce books that children want to read again and again.

Dr. Peg Ballard
Mankato State University

# Photo Credits

All photos © copyright: Dembinsky Photo Associates: 9; PhotoEdit: 16 (Myrleen Ferguson); Photri, Inc.: 5, 6, 12 (J. Novak), 15; Tony Stone Images: 2 (Tim Davis), 10 (Renee Lynn), 19 (Don Smetzer), 20 (Walter Hodges). Cover: Tony Stone/Lori Adamski Peek.

An Editorial Directions Book
Photo Research: Alice Flanagan
Design and production: Herman Adler Design Group

Library of Congress Cataloging-in-Publication Data

Flanagan, Alice K.
    Dogs : the sound of "d" / by Alice K. Flanagan.
       p. cm. — (Wonder books)
    Summary : Simple text and repetition of the letter "d" help readers learn how to use this sound.
    ISBN 1-56766-694-9 (lib. bdg. : alk. paper)
    [1. Dogs Fiction. 2. Alphabet.] I. Title. II. Series: Wonder books (Chanhassen, Minn.)
PZ7.F59824Do    1999
[E]—dc21
                                                    99-20964
                                                        CIP

11/99